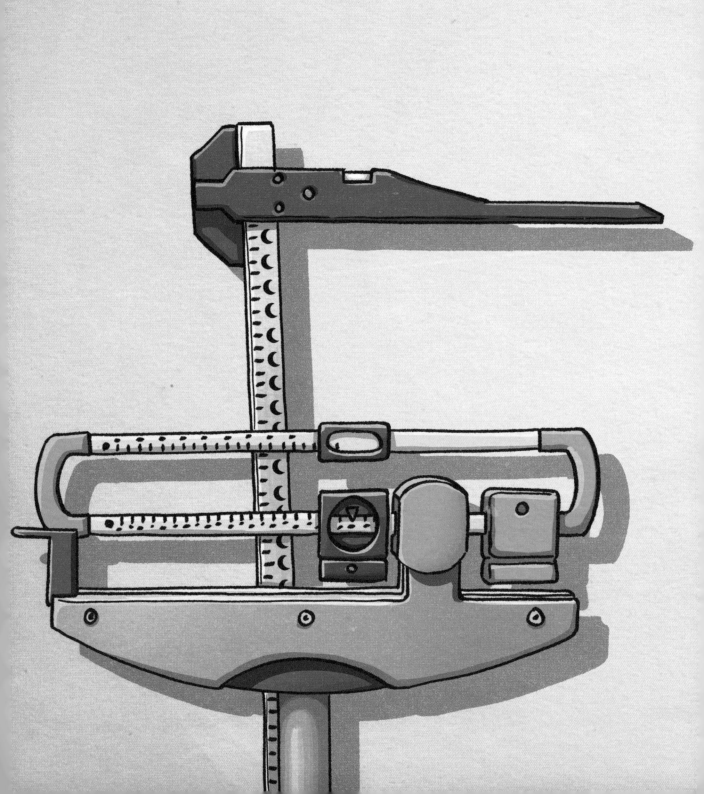

For the little kids still kidding
around, no matter where they are . . .

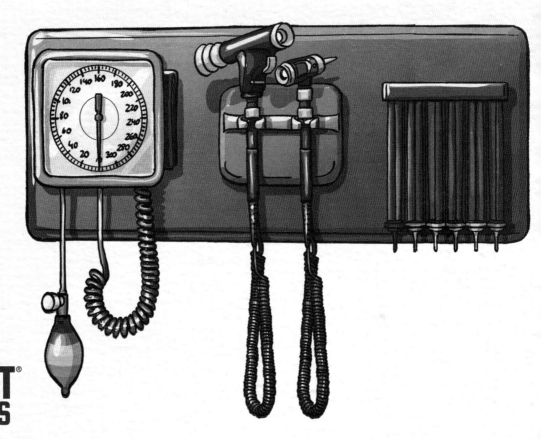

MASCOT ® **BOOKS**

www.mascotbooks.com

ADVENTURES AT THE HOSPITAL

For more information, please contact:
Mascot Books
620 Herndon Parkway, Suite 320
Herndon, VA 20170
info@mascotbooks.com

Library of Congress Control Number: 2020924215

CPSIA Code: PRT1220A
ISBN-13: 978-1-64543-891-5

Printed in the United States

ADVENTURES AT THE HOSPITAL

Michael Ban

Illustrated by
Walter Policelli

This is a story about little boys and little girls making little visits to the hospital.

The hospital is a place full of wonderful wonders . . .

Where supremely smart people use their superpowers to help us feel *SUPER.*

Before little boys and little girls are admitted to the hospital, they must put on their super-grip slippers so they do not slip on the slippery hospital floors!

Next, little boys and little girls have to put on special capes to keep them clean.

Now that the kids are wearing what they need to wear, the nurses start nursing . . .

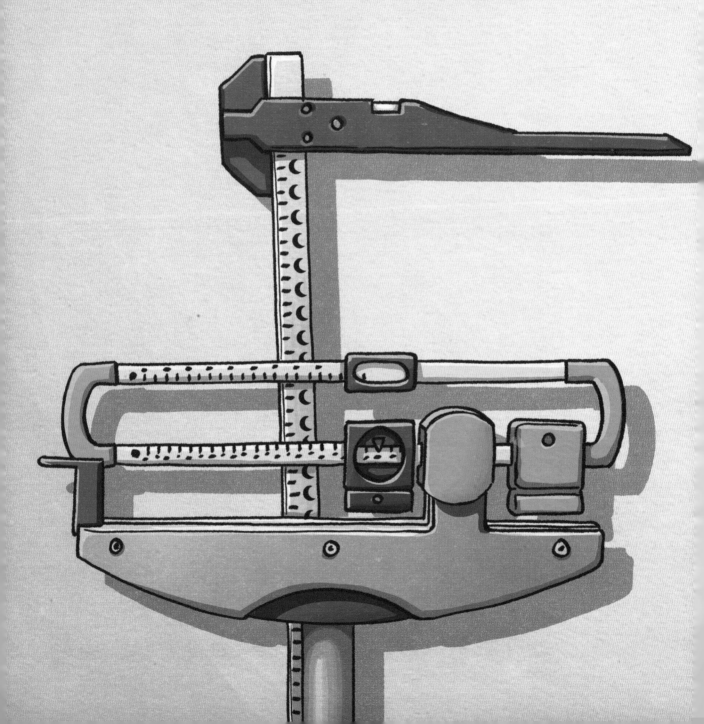

. . . by measuring all the necessary measurements!

Height: to see how close they are to the moon!

Weight: to see how big their cannonball splashes would be!

Arms: to see how strong they are!

Now that the nurses have learned how close to the moon the kids stand, the size of their cannonball splashes, and their arm strength, it is time to climb into the funny music machine that goes *EEEEEEH* and *ERRRRRRRR* and *KUHH CHUNK CHUNKKKK!*

Finally, the doctor arrives and takes one last measurement to see if the patients have the courage to be courageous! She listens to their hearts going *BA BUMP, BA BUMP!*

After all the checks check out, it's time for little boys and girls to head back home where their family and friends are all together, happily being happy . . .

together . . . forever!

CAN YOU FIND THE FOLLOWING OBJECTS HIDDEN IN THIS ADVENTURE?

ABOUT THE AUTHOR

Michael Ban is a brain cancer survivor and children's hospital alumnus who has many fond memories of the people he met through his experiences at the hospital—as a patient, friend, family member, friend of a family member, family member of a friend, or visitor! Michael works as a healthcare attorney for a major hospital system when he is not writing short stories and poems, or FaceTiming with his favorite niece, Parker (who, coincidentally, is also his only niece).